Stand Beautiful

written by **Chloe Howard** illustrated by **Deborah Melmon**

 ZONDER**kidz**

How you made me is amazing and wonderful.
I praise you for that. What you have done is wonderful.

—Psalm 139:14

For all my friends, young and old: Stand Beautiful, and be bold.

—CH

For Adi and Nolie

—DM

ZONDERKIDZ

Stand Beautiful

Copyright © 2018 by Chloe Howard
Illustrations © 2018 Deborah Melmon Illustration

Requests for information should be addressed to:
Zonderkidz, 3900 Sparks Drive SE, Grand Rapids, Michigan 49546

ISBN 978-0-310-76495-3

Published in association with the literary agency of Mark Oestreicher.

Zonderkidz is a trademark of Zondervan.

Contributor: Jill Gorey
Design: Cindy Davis

Printed in China

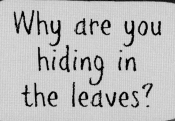

I feel so happy, I want to tell the world!
WOO HOO! Road trip!
LET'S DO IT!
STAND BEAUTIFUL!

YOU DESERVE
TO BE LOVED
JUST AS YOU ARE!
STAND BEAUTIFUL!
I can
dig it!

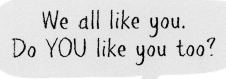

IFUL!
Don't forget, sometimes our differences are on the inside.
I never learned how to hop.
I'm not good at reading.
I'm shy.
I'm a vegetarian.
I'm not good at fetch.

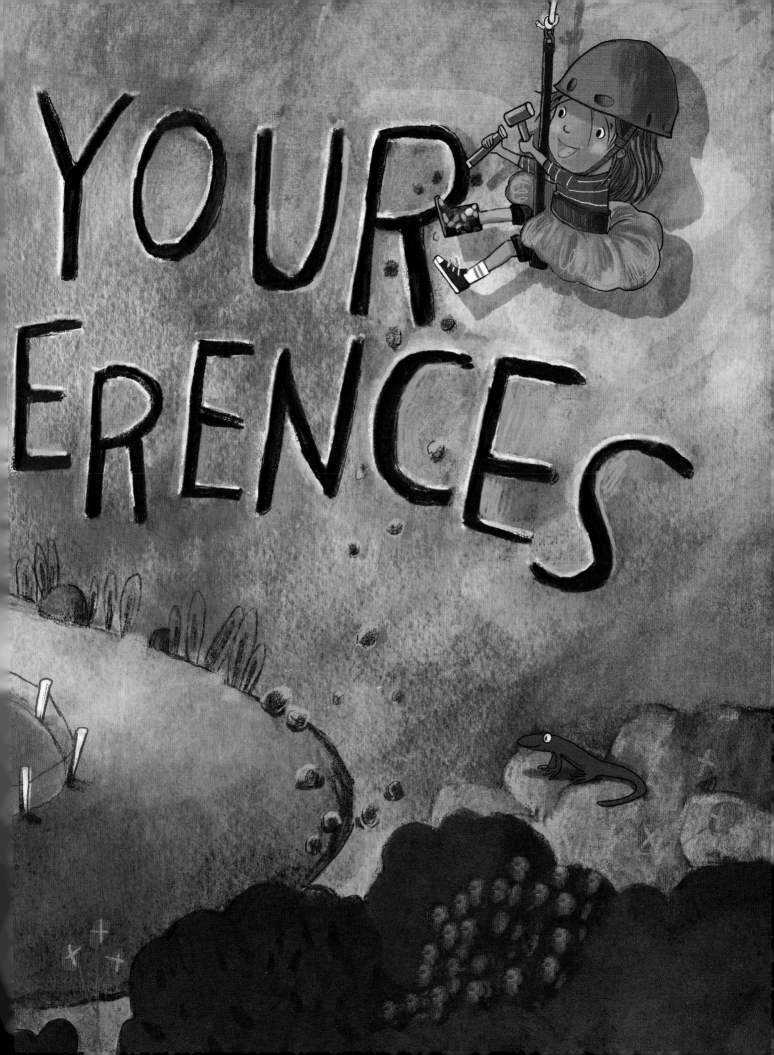

Well, I know something you're great at ...
You're GREAT at being YOU.

I AM the best ME there is!

WE'RE FIRED UP,
WE'RE SIZZLING,
WE'RE TURNING UP THE HEAT!
AND WHEN WE ALL STAND BEAUTIFUL
THIS TEAM JUST CAN'T BE BEAT!
Stand Beautiful!
Stand Beautiful!

Dear Reader,

I hope when the Stand Beautiful bus comes along, you hop right on!

Keep on encouraging people and helping them love themselves; let's build each other up!

Remember that you are perfect just the way you are—you don't have to be anyone but YOU!

I hope you can see yourself just as Jesus sees you:

Beautiful! Awesome! Brave! Unique!

Don't be afraid to let your true colors SHINE!

Stand Beautiful with me!

Love,

Chloe

beautiful.chloehoward.com